WISE OWL'S STORY

Uniform with this volume:

Wise Owl's Story

by Alison Uttley
Pictures by
Margaret Tempest

Collins

William Collins Sons & Co Ltd
London · Glasgow · Sydney · Auckland
Toronto · Johannesburg

First impression 1935
This edition 1978
Copyright reserved
ISBN 0 00 194102 X
Made and Printed in Great Britain by
William Collins Sons & Co Ltd Glasgow

FOREWORD

OF course you must understand that Grey Rabbit's home had no electric light or gas, and even the candles were made from pith of rushes dipped in wax from the wild bees' nests, which Squirrel found. Water there was in plenty, but it did not come from a tap. It flowed from a spring outside, which rose up from the ground and went to a brook. Grey Rabbit cooked on a fire, but it was a wood fire, there was no coal in that part of the country. Tea did not come from India, but from a little herb known very well to country people, who once dried it and used it in their cottage homes. Bread was baked from wheat ears, ground fine, and Hare and Grey Rabbit gleaned in the cornfields to get the wheat.

The doormats were plaited rushes, like country-made mats, and cushions were stuffed with wool gathered from the hedges where sheep pushed through the thorns. As for the looking-glass, Grey Rabbit found the glass, dropped from a lady's handbag, and Mole made a frame for it. Usually the animals gazed at themselves in the still pools as so many country children have done. The country ways of Grey Rabbit were the country ways known to the author.

WISE OWL lived in the hollow oak tree in the middle of the wood. Anyone could see it was Wise Owl's house, for a little silver bell with an eagle on it, and curly lines like a shell round its edges, hung beside the front door. There were windows high up in the tree, hidden in the rough bark, and a wisp of blue smoke came out of the chimney, among the leaves, when Owl was at home.

THE HOUSE WAS VERY OLD and very untidy. Dust and dirt of ages filled the rooms, and cobwebs hung in festoons from the ceilings. Sometimes bits of tree fell into the soup when Wise Owl was cooking, but he was too wise a bird to mind, and he stirred them about with his wooden spoon, murmuring, " How interesting! "

" A morsel of a house which has lasted since Queen Elizabeth's time gives a tasty flavour to the broth! "

THERE WERE little attics and storerooms all over the tree, filled with lumber and old wood, and spiders. Wise Owl never went into these rooms, for he kept to his kitchen, his bedroom, and his study.

In the bedroom there was a little four-poster, with a small carved owl perched on each bed-post, and on it lay a goose-feather bed. In the kitchen was a frying-pan, but in the study were all Owl's books of wisdom. Round the walls were shelves, and there the books were arranged, books in green, brown, and beautiful red bindings, exactly the same colours as the leaves of the trees.

The books of poetry and rhyme were green, like the young leaves of Spring.

THOSE ON HISTORY and arithmetic were brown, like the dead leaves of winter, and the story books were *red* (which is an Owlish joke). Owl had always loved reading, ever since he was a small Owlet, and had peered, one moonlight night, through the window of a museum. He had seen, in a glass case, a Greek coin with an owl upon it, and he knew he was a bird of wisdom.

ONE EVENING, just as dusk fell, Owl yawned and got down from his easy-chair, where he had been dozing. He sniffed at the cool air which came through the window. The wind had changed, and there was a strange rippling motion which he felt at once in his feathers.

"A storm's brewing somewhere," said he to himself. "There will be a gale to-night. I must shut the windows before I go out, or my books will get wet."

He took down his weather book, and turned the pages, which fluttered in the breeze like the leaves in the trees around. He sat down in the doorway and read some wisdom about cyclones and rain-drops, and he nodded his wise old head as he read.

THEN HE TOOK a sip of little Grey Rabbit's primrose wine, and watched the moon sail in the night sky among great ragged black clouds. The clouds came hurrying up, whipped by the rising wind, and Wise Owl flew off over the woods and fields. He had to go far that night before he found his supper.

The wind whirled through the wood in a fury. It tossed the trees and snapped the branches. It rattled and banged at the doors and windows of all the little houses in the fields and hedgerows. It screamed through the key-holes, and whistled down the chimneys, and shook the tiny doors.

MOLE, in his underground house, knew nothing of the storm. He lay under his blanket, dreaming of music and songs, but Mrs. Hedgehog awoke her husband in the cottage close by.

"There's a crash!" said she. "Get up, Hedgehog, and see what's the matter. I believe our house has blown down."

Old Hedgehog crawled sleepily to the window, and stared out. On the ground under the hedge was a little hollow chimney, rolling about among the leaves.

"Th' chimbley's come off," said he. "It was a great noise for our little chimbley."

"WHAT SHALL WE DO? Suppose the house blows away?" cried Mrs. Hedgehog, clutching the bedside.

"Our house is safe enough, wife," answered Hedgehog. "It's the big things that goes in a storm. Church steeples, and great trees, not tiddley houses like ours, close to the ground. That chimbley would never have been blowed off it if hadn't been stuck up. A good riddance!" He climbed back to bed and fell asleep in spite of Mrs. Hedgehog's protests.

The sound of the wind and the echo of a crash awoke Hare, in the little house at the end of the wood.

"My goodness! It will blow my whiskers off," he cried, and he pulled the bedclothes over his long ears.

SQUIRREL SHIVERED and curled her tail closely round her shoulders. Little Grey Rabbit in her attic opened her eyes, and listened to the creaking of the trees in the wood. After a time she heard a strange wailing voice which seemed to come from somewhere near.

" Too-whit, too-whoo! I've lost my ho-o-ome! " moaned through the night air, but when she sat up in bed she heard nothing except the screech of the wind. " I was dreaming," said she.

When Wise Owl's hunting was over, he tried to fly back to his tree, but the wind blew him out of his path, and he was very tired with buffeting against the blast. He knew the wood so well he could find his way home blindfolded, so, with his eyes half-shut, he blundered on towards his front door.

BUT IT WASN'T THERE! He gasped with surprise, and circled round, but there was no silver bell, no little brown door, no great oak tree!

"Am I bewitched?" said he. "Have I come to the wrong wood?" He flew among the tree-tops and found the familiar outlines, the plumes and tufts and spires of the trees he knew. Then he looked down to the ground, and he saw the oak tree stretched there like a fallen giant. The door was broken off, books lay scattered on the grass, a dictionary floated like a white lily on a pool of rain-water, and the silver bell had gone.

"OH WOE! WOE IS ME!"
cried the Owl. "Too-Whit! To-
Whoo! What shall I do?" His great
wisdom deserted him, and he was just
a lonely unhappy owl, very wet and
very tired, with no home to rest in.

The wind screamed with glee, and
tossed his books about, wetting the
tiny pages, blowing them about like
dandelion clocks. The trees swished
him with their wet branches, lashed
him with stinging whips, and he had
no shelter. He rose up and flapped his
way over the wood, and it was then
that little Grey Rabbit heard his plain-
tive cry.

THE NEXT MORNING the gale dropped, but the rain poured down. The little rabbit could hear the patter of the drops on the roof as she dressed, and she looked from her window at a drenched world.

" I wonder what that crash was I heard in the night," said she to herself. " I'll just slip out while the others are asleep. I want to wear my new goloshes."

She brought out her shiny goloshes from the hole under the stairs. She bent them backwards and forwards like willow saplings, and sniffed at the nice smell.

WHERE DID THEY come from? Nobody knew. They appeared on the doorstep one morning, with " A Present for Grey Rabbit " written on a holly leaf, but Mole and Hedgehog had never even heard of them. The strange thing was that it had never rained since they came, so little Grey Rabbit was glad to wear them. She slipped a cloak over her shoulders and ran out in the wet, down the path to the wood.

" My feet are quite dry! " she exclaimed, as she paddled through a pool, and she paddled back again, just to feel like a duck.

WHEN SHE GOT NEAR Wise Owl's house, she saw the fallen tree and the broken door and all the tumbled wet books.

"Oh! Poor Wise Owl! What will he do with no home!" she cried, and she gathered up some of the books, and put them under the tree for shelter.

She looked round for Wise Owl, but he was nowhere to be seen, so she hurried back with her sad news.

"We must all do something," said Hare, as he ate his porridge.

"Yes, let's do something really useful," said Squirrel, and she sipped daintily at her tea.

"SHOULD WE INVITE HIM here as our guest till he finds another house?" asked Grey Rabbit.

"Here?" exclaimed Hare, puckering up his face. "In this house, Grey Rabbit? Are you mad?"

"He'd break our cups with his wings," said Squirrel. "He'd be asleep all day, when we wanted to tidy the house, and make the beds. Besides, his ways are not our ways." She shivered.

"No, it wouldn't do," agreed Grey Rabbit. "He must have a house of his own. The little birds will mob him if they see him. It isn't right for a respectable old wiseacre like Owl to be pecked and teased by jeering common sparrows and jays.

"HE MUST have a nice big house to hold all those books of wisdom which I saw lying in the rain."

There was silence for a moment, and then Grey Rabbit said, " Suppose we go out and look for one for him."

" Can't he do that himself? " grumbled Squirrel.

" He doesn't like the daylight, you know, and at night he is too busy," said Grey Rabbit. " We will wait till the rain stops, and then we will take sandwiches and spend the day house-hunting."

" Sandwiches?   Splendid! " cried Hare. " I love house-hunting! " He ran to the door and looked out.

" There's a rainbow in the sky, Grey Rabbit. We can go quite soon."

THE THREE ANIMALS set out on their expedition through the wood, but although they looked to the right and the left, high up and low down, they couldn't find a hollow tree.

Squirrel jumped among the tree-tops, and Hare leaped high on the ground, and little Grey Rabbit ran with her nose in the air, sniffing and hunting, but there didn't seem to be a house to spare anywhere.

They took their sandwiches out of their pockets and sat down to eat them near the fallen tree. Grey Rabbit fished the little dictionary out of the pool, and wiped it on her handkerchief. Squirrel found a book of nursery songs in a briar bush. Hare picked up a history book, but that was quite dry.

"I WONDER WHERE Wise Owl is," said Grey Rabbit, and she peeped through the door into the dusty rooms. " I hope he hasn't flown away to another country."

" He's somewhere about," said Hare placidly. " I don't want to see him."

" He is as dull as this history book." He flung it into the pond, where it lay, still dry.

" Let us all go different ways," said Squirrel. " Then if we haven't found a house by tea-time, we will go home."

" And have plum cake for tea," sighed Hare hungrily.

" And hot buttered toast," said Squirrel.

Hare tossed a straw in the air, to see which way he should go, and then he set off down an inviting little green path.

HE SOON FOUND HIMSELF
out of the wood, in a wet green
meadow. There in the grass grew
round, white satiny knobs.

" Mushrooms! " he cried, and he
filled his pockets. He forgot all about
Wise Owl's house as he wandered
about the field. At the gate he met
an elderly rabbit, leaning on a crutch,
and they stood talking of the storm.

" Such a wind! It blew the garden
gate off its hinges," said the rabbit,
" and I hobbled in for my breakfast.
I haven't had such a feast since my
accident. ' It's an ill wind that blows
nobody good,' as my father used to
say."

" Is the gate still down? " asked
Hare.

"OH YES. There's plenty left," replied the rabbit. Hare thanked him, gave him a pawful of mushrooms, and then ran with his long legs across the fields to the farm garden.

Squirrel started off along a little path in the opposite direction, but soon she saw a hazel tree with round brown nuts clustering upon it. She sprang up the boughs, and feasted, cracking the shells and nibbling the sweet kernels.

" Ah! Why can't I come here every day? " she asked herself. She went a little farther and came to a mountain ash.

UP SHE RAN, and rubbed her cheeks against the scarlet berries. She picked a bunch, and threaded them on a grass. Then she hung them round her neck, and gazed at herself in a pool of rain water.

" Scarlet suits me," said she, simpering, and she certainly looked very pretty with her necklace.

A silver birch stood in her path, and she stood before the lovely white tree, with its tiny pointed leaves. She stripped off a piece of the bark, and wound it round her paws.

" Grey Rabbit's slippers are made of silver birch, those the Toad sent to her," she mused. She tried to weave a pair for her own tiny feet, but it was more difficult than she supposed, and she flung the silken strips away.

THEN SHE RAN up the tree
and sported herself on the delicate sprays of green.

" It's like a roundabout at the fair,"
said she, swinging to and fro. " Lulla-
lullaby," she sang, and she rocked
herself up and down till the tree shook
with her antics.

Then she curled up in a corner and
went to sleep, for the leaves were
fragrant, and the branch was soft.
She forgot all about Wise Owl and
his home, as she lay curled up high
in the air. When she awoke it was
too late to bother, and she gaily
danced her way home.

LITTLE GREY RABBIT ran along the path to the West, looking to right and left for a hollow tree. She dodged in and out, sniffing and searching, and she marked each tree with a tiny white cross, so that none should be overlooked.

She worked so hard she did not notice that the afternoon had passed, and evening was approaching. She tapped the trees, and marked them, moving farther and farther from home, until at last she heard the sound she had been listening for all day.

She stopped in front of a great beech tree and tapped again. It was hollow!

HERE WAS A HOUSE for Wise Owl! She ran round the trunk and pulled away the brambles and leaves which concealed the opening. Then, rather frightened, she went inside.

There was a splendid empty house! It was rather damp, of course, but a little fire would soon dry it. There were three rooms, and lots of attics, and shelves all round the walls. It was just right for Wise Owl.

She went to the door and looked out.

The moon was rising behind the hill, and a soft golden glow spread over the wood. A moonbeam shone into the doorway, and lighted up a pool of water on the ground.

GREY RABBIT thought of Wise
Owl just starting on his rounds,
and she felt frightened. She thought
of her home, and the supper table,
and bright fire, the ticking clock, and
the cosy hearth, and she felt very
lonely. She didn't know where she
was, and there was nothing to be
done, except to stay there all night.

She picked up a tiny glow-worm
and carried it in with her. Then she
pulled some wood across the doorway, to keep out foxes, and stoats,
and savage beasts, which might roam
through the wood at night.

She climbed on to a rough shelf,
made herself as small as possible, and
fell asleep, with the glow-worm shining
like a little night-light.

WHEN HARE HAD EATEN half the lettuce bed he went home, and there he found Squirrel who sat with her necklace round her neck, rocking herself backwards and forwards, and reading one of Owl's books.

" I got here first," she said. " I won the prize."

" What prize? " asked Hare.

" The prize for getting here first. The mushrooms," said she.

" How did you know? " asked the bewildered Hare, emptying his pockets.

" By the knobs in your coat," said Squirrel calmly.

" Where is little Grey Rabbit? " asked Hare. " Hasn't she come home yet? "

" No, she probably met Wise Owl, and they talked about tails and bells,

and hollow trees," said Squirrel. "She'll come soon."

They had tea without her, but when supper-time came, and there was no little Grey Rabbit, they both grew anxious.

Hare put a lighted candle in the window to light her home, and then he stood at the door and called, " Coo-ee. Coo-ee. Coo-ee." His voice rang through the air, but there was no answer.

" Coo-ee. Coo-ee." he called again, and " Too-Whit, Too-Whoo," a shrill voice hooted nearby.

Hare started. Who was that? Where did that noise come from?

Wise Owl came out of the wood-shed, yawning with wide open mouth.

" Did you call? " he asked coolly.

" WE'VE LOST GREY RABBIT,"
explained Hare nervously.

" What is she doing out late like this? " asked the Owl.

" She is looking for a house for you."

" A house for me? " echoed Wise Owl. " I am going to live in your wood-shed. It is warm and comfortable, and there is plenty of food about."

He stepped into the house and snapped up all the mushrooms and hot buttered toast which lay ready for supper.

Squirrel dived under a chair and lay there shaking with fright. Hare fidgeted on one leg, and said nothing.

" I'D BETTER GO OFF and find Grey Rabbit," said Wise Owl. " You stay here, and wait up for her. You'd be lost if you came too." He flew off with his ghost-like flight, a silently moving shadow, and Hare mopped his brow.

" Whew! " he cried. " I did feel nervous. I never thought I should live to see the day when an Owl would come into the kitchen and eat my supper before my very eyes! "

" Better to eat your supper, than to eat you," said Squirrel, crawling from under the chair. " He's been eating the mice in the wood-shed all day, or he might have gobbled you, Hare."

" Stuff and nonsense," said Hare, and he sat down to wait for the Owl's return.

WISE OWL flew over the woods, calling, but either the tree was too thick or Grey Rabbit was too fast asleep, she never heard his voice, and he had to return without her.

"She's lost!" he said huskily. "Little Grey Rabbit's gone. I asked Rat, who thumped along the hedge-side with that knot in his tail, but he hadn't seen her. I asked the stoat, and several other night people, but no one had seen her."

Hare and Squirrel were very much alarmed, for Wise Owl was a famous finder of lost animals.

"I am going to sleep now," said he. "Don't disturb me. You two must go out and look for her. The morning's here, and Hedgehog the milkman is starting on his rounds. I saw him

trying to put a broken chimney on his roof. I ordered an extra jug of milk for myself."

"Now hurry up," commanded the Owl, as he stood in the doorway. "No dilly-dallying! No shilly-shally-ing! Turn up your sleeves, Hare, and take that necklace from your neck, Squirrel. Off you go to look for your companion!"

The two animals sprang up, and got ready, with sticks and map and com-pass, and Owl returned to the wood-shed.

"He orders us about as if he lived here," complained Squirrel. "Oh, I do wish Grey Rabbit would come back!"

THERE WAS A sound outside, the door was pushed open, and in came little Grey Rabbit, looking as fresh as a daisy. She had washed in a stream, and brushed her hair with a teasel brush.

" Wherever have you been? " cried Hare. " We were just going to look for you. Owl was hunting for you all night."

Little Grey Rabbit turned pale.

" To find you, not to eat you," said Hare crossly. " We never went to bed, and here you are looking as if you had been enjoying yourself."

" I am so sorry," said Grey Rabbit humbly. " I got lost. I must have walked in a circle, for I was really quite near Owl's old tree, and I didn't know. I found a home for Owl! "

"THANK GOODNESS," exclaimed Hare, and he flung himself on the rocking chair with relief. Then he hesitated.

"Is it a nice house, Grey Rabbit? Owl is in the wood-shed, and he won't go away unless it is a nicer house than ours."

"Couldn't we spring-clean it for him, whilst he is asleep, and put his books inside, and then he will want to go?" asked Squirrel.

"Oh yes," cried Grey Rabbit, who loved to polish and scrub. "But I am so hungry.

"I had nothing to eat last night, and this morning there wasn't time to stop."

"Owl ate our supper last night," said Hare gloomily, "but luckily he didn't notice the larder door."

SQUIRREL hustled round, and soon a plate of porridge and treacle was ready for the rabbit.

They then took buckets and mops and scrubbing brushes and soap, and walked off to the wood.

Grey Rabbit led them to a beautiful beech tree, with golden brown leaves spreading in a tent overhead, and thousands of beech-nuts hanging from the branches, and spilling on the warm earth.

" I shouldn't mind living here myself," said Squirrel as she cracked the three-cornered nuts and ate the tiny kernels. " We will take some of these home for beech-bread."

" It's a fine tree," said Hare, " but where is the door? " Grey Rabbit pointed out the small hole near the ground.

"OWL WON'T WANT to fly down to the earth when he comes home," objected Hare. "I don't think he will change from the wood-shed."

Then he added hurriedly, "Excuse me a moment. I've forgotten something. I must run home," and away he went.

"He doesn't want to scrub and rub," said Squirrel crossly, but Grey Rabbit took her into the tree, and she forgot her disapproval of Hare as she explored the rooms.

"It's a very nice house," said she, "fit for a king."

They filled their buckets from the pool near-by, and they scrubbed and mopped the floors and walls and ceilings. They washed the little shelves and book-cases, and the cupboards which hung all round the tree.

"I DO LIKE plenty of cupboards," sighed Grey Rabbit happily, as she fastened a knob on the door.

They beeswaxed the shelves, and lined them with fresh beech-leaves, and they hung a bunch of wild thyme on a wooden nail to make a sweet smell.

"Owl will be able to keep all his books here," said Squirrel and she put some pointed chestnut leaves on the floor for green carpets. "There's a place for his blotting-paper, and his pen and ink, and——"

"Tape measure and thimble," interrupted a voice, and Hare came in carrying a saw.

"What's that for?" asked Squirrel.

"It's a saw to saw things," said Hare. "You never thought, but I did."

HE SAT DOWN on a bench and folded his arms.

"Do you imagine that Wise Owl would live here with that door? Why, he couldn't get through it without crawling! I could scarcely get my ears inside, and he would have to leave his wings in the wood!" Hare laughed and went on, "I said to myself, 'That Owl will want to live in our wood-shed if we don't do something.' So I'm going to make a door, high up, so that he can fly right in, and no burglars can get to his rooms."

He climbed up the steep stairs, and cut a neat door in the tree.

HE FASTENED hinges of springy bark, so that no one would notice it. Then he cut a window in Owl's study, which was very dark and dismal, and put another in the kitchen.

" A nice airy house with every modern convenience," said he proudly, as he stepped backwards to view his work, but he trod on the soap and fell downstairs to the bottom of the tree.

" The proper place to keep soap is the larder, so put it there," cried he, rubbing his head, and calling up to Squirrel. " Never leave soap on the stairs, Squirrel." So Squirrel placed it on the larder shelf.

The three animals went to the oak tree and collected the books, which were now dry with the wind and the sun.

THEY CARRIED THEM across to the new house, and arranged them on the shelves. They picked up Owl's cuckoo clock which hung in a bush. " Cuckoo! Cuckoo! Cuckoo! " it struck.

" Is this one of Owl's magics? " cried Squirrel. " I wondered why the first cuckoo was always heard in this wood! " They hung it on the staircase, and returned for Owl's rush-bottomed chair, and three-legged stool, his feather-bed and frying-pan. Hare found the sealing-wax, and Squirrel the candlestick, and little Grey Rabbit found Owl's night-cap dangling in the nettles, but nowhere could they see the little silver bell.

" Moley's bell," sighed little Grey Rabbit. " It was such a beautiful bell, and it saved my tail. I do hope it will turn up."

THEY ALL HUNTED round the wood for house-warming presents for the Owl, to welcome him when he came to his new home. Hare picked a robin's red pin-cushion, to hold Owl's needles and pins. Squirrel got a piece of honeycomb from a wild bees' nest. Little Grey Rabbit gathered some starry moss, for a green cushion.

The house was finished and they stood in the grass staring up and admiring the shiny grey trunk of the tree, and the sloping boughs with the little door hidden among them, when Hedgehog walked up.

" Hello! " said he. " I've just found Owl's bell. I was walking along the path through the wood, looking for a new chimbley for our house, when I heard a tinkly tinkle, and there was a

mouse playing with Owl's bell! Did you ever hear the like? A mouse with Owl's bell! "

" A bold mouse! " said Hare. " Luckily for him, Owl is asleep in our wood-shed."

He explained the disasters of the night of the storm.

Hedgehog nodded. " Just what I told my Missus," said he. " Great oaks fall and little acorns weather the gale."

Little Grey Rabbit took the silver bell and examined it. It was none the worse but she rubbed it, and polished it.

Then Squirrel ran up the tree and hung it at the side of Owl's front door. and the four walked back to the little house at the edge of the wood.

"WAKE UP, WISE OWL," they cried, tapping on his door. "Wake up. There's a new house for you in the wood."

"Don't want a new house," muttered Wise Owl sleepily. "Go away and play."

"Your books are on the shelves," said Hare.

"Your cuckoo clock's ticking on the stairs," said Squirrel.

"Your night-cap is on the bed," said Grey Rabbit.

"Your bell's a-tinkling by the front door," said Hedgehog.

Wise Owl came out and blinked at them.

"**D**ID YOU SAY you had put my tree up again?" he asked.

"No. We've found another, a better one," said little Grey Rabbit.

Without another word Wise Owl flew off, flapping silently away in the daylight, never heeding the crowd of small birds which followed after. They twittered and cried, but Owl saw the silver bell, and he pushed open the door. He walked upstairs, one step at a time, and he looked in all the cupboards and on the shelves. He counted his books, and only one was missing —the nursery songs which Squirrel had taken home with her, but Owl knew those ditties by heart.

HE THREW OPEN the round window which Hare had made, and looked at the great roof of the tree above him. He ran his beak over the smooth floor, and smelled the sweet sawdust which lay in a pile on the floor.

" A pinch of a house that was here in King Charles's time gives a sharp relish to the broth," said he, and he carried the little heap to the larder, ready for his soup-making. Then he saw the delicate honeycomb and the cake of soap.

" The honey I'll keep for to-morrow, but this cake will do for my supper before I go hunting."

HE SWALLOWED IT, and snapped his beak.

"Tasty! A tasty morsel!" said he. "That was somebody's kind thought! I must give a present each to the Squirrel, the Hare and the little Grey Rabbit. They've certainly done me a good turn. Something for something has always been Owl's motto."

He searched in his treasure box, which was buried deep in the brown leaf-mould of the wood, and he took them—what do you think?

A tiny basket, carved out of a cherry stone; a sailing boat, made from half a walnut-shell; a little beech-tree growing out of a beech-nut! Now can you guess which had which?

The End of the Story

For Ruthie
Love from
Mummy
& Daddy.
x x x x x x
Christmas
1983.

margaret Tempest.